SUPER CEO GIRLS

BOOK 1

The Case of the Doctor Dilemma

Written by

Audrey K. Chisholm

To Alejandra, Annalisa, Adrianna, and Juan Phillip II.
Always remember that you are smart, you are leaders, you are business owners, you are children of God, and you are going to change the world.
And remember Philippians 4:13.

- Audrey K. Chisholm

Noble Strength Enterprises, LLC, Florida

Text and Illustrations Copyright © 2022 by Audrey K. Chisholm.

All rights reserved.

Visit us online at
www.superceogirls.com

Printed in the United States of America

"DINNERTIME!"

Kate, Lisa, and Anna raced down the spiral staircase of their mansion. Halfway down, Kate tripped and tumbled to the bottom.

"Not again," said Anna. "Are you OK?"

Kate laughed. "I'm fine!"

Anna reached out to help Kate up. "You've lived here for eight years and you still can't come down the steps without tripping."

She laughed.

"I know," said Kate. "I guess **all my superpowers are in my brains**, not my legs."

"Come to the table, girls," said Mom.

Kate, Lisa, and Anna kissed their mom and dad before taking their seats at the dining room table.

Mom turned to the butler, who was waiting at the end of the table in a black suit and white gloves.

"Barnaby, what's for dinner tonight?"

Barnaby the butler cleared his throat. "For your pleasure tonight, ladies and gentleman, we will have Beef Wellington with a side of warm wilted wintergreens and garlic and herb roasted potatoes."

"Sounds yummy," said Anna.

"Sounds yucky! Wilted greens and herby potatoes?" said Lisa. "Can I have pizza?"

"Not today," said Mom. "But you can try your greens **with an open mind.** I think you'll like them."

"That will be five Beef Wellingtons and one with extra greens for Miss Lisa," Barnaby said with a wink and picked up a bell and rang it.

As the kitchen staff brought the meals, the girls' baby brother started crying. Dad got up. "I'm going to change baby John. Excuse me, folks. I'll be right back."

"Sure, honey," Mom answered. "Girls, I hope you have been paying attention to your dad and me so that you can grow up and **run businesses of your own someday.**"

"Yes, ma'am," said Kate.

She looked over at her sisters and winked her eye.

"What do I always tell you?" Mom asked.

The girls spoke in unison. **"Dream it, do it, don't give up!"**

After dinner, Mom put her napkin on the table. "I've got a few phone calls to make on a big deal I'm working on. Then we will have story time, OK?"

"OK, Mom," said Anna.

As soon as Mom and Dad left the room, Kate jumped up.
"**Come on, girls! We've got our own work to do!**"

They rushed into the playroom and closed the door. When they were sure Mom and Dad could not see or hear them, Kate gave the order.

"The lair, Lisa."

Lisa pressed a large red button on the wall. The walls slid up, revealing the Super CEO Girls' secret headquarters.

Kate rushed over to Communication Station and began typing. Five huge computer screens hung on the wall in front of her. They made lots of beeping sounds as they scanned the world for kids in business who **might need their help.**

"What area are you working on, Kate?" asked Lisa.

"I'm checking the eastern sector," said Kate. "We haven't been there in a while. Maybe there is a kid with a business we can help. I checked it earlier. There just don't seem to be any businesses in trouble today."

"There are always businesses that need our superpowers. Check one more time, pleeeeease," said Lisa, laughing. "I'm pumped!"

"I'll check!" said Anna with a big smile.

She ran over to the Communication Station.
But before she got there . . . a blaring alarm filled the room, and a bright red light in the ceiling spun around and around.

"Yay!" shouted Lisa. "That's the Notifier. That means there is a business out there in trouble. Come on, Super CEO Girls. It's time to do our thing!"

"Bracelets on!" Anna said.

They each pressed the power button on their glittery bracelets.

"Advertising Power!" said Kate as she raised her arm with her pink bracelet to the sky.

"Piggy Bank Power!" said Lisa as she lifted up her arm with a gold bracelet.

"People Power!" said Anna as she raised her arm up with her green bracelet.

"Bracelets in," said Kate.

They stacked their hands, one on top of the other. This caused their bracelets to glow. Bright lights and popping sparkles filled the room as the girls rose up in the air.

Then *poof!* They were transformed into the **Super CEO Girls.**

Their capes glittered with pink and gold.

"Let's join hands and say the Super CEO Girl pledge to take us to the kid in trouble," said Kate.

They held hands and shouted:

"Super CEOs.

We're smart, don't you know?

Our bracelets are aglow,

And . . . now . . . it's . . . time . . . to . . . GO!!"

They opened their eyes to find themselves floating in the air above Kidtropolis.

"There!" said Kate, pointing to the small town of Hopesville.

Anna and Lisa lowered themselves to the ground, landing as soft as feathers. But Kate tumbled and rolled toward the bushes.

"Are you OK?" Anna asked.

"I'm OK!" said Kate with a laugh. "Let's go, CEOs. Somewhere nearby, there is a kid with a business that's in trouble."

"I love helping people," Anna said with a shy giggle, "even though it means meeting someone new."

"It's alright!" said Kate. "Meeting someone new means a chance to make a friend!"

"I'm ready," said Lisa.

"Let's go, girls!" said Kate.

Meanwhile, in the center of Hopesville, kids ran all types of businesses. Kids were in charge of every restaurant, bookstore, and mechanic shop.

A girl named **Dr. Emma** was standing in front of her office. She glanced up and down the street with a sad look on her face.

Her doctor's office was bright and beautiful. But she had no patients to treat.

Just then, a red bear with a mean face came walking up to her. He was about the same size as Dr. Emma.

Where his left eye had once been, there were two bandages in a crisscross shape. He had little scars on his face and paws, and he was wearing the sourest expression.

Over his head, a thick black cloud of smoke swirled around and around. Across his chest was a money bag. He blinked his beady eye at Dr. Emma and growled at her fiercely.

"Uh, hi," said Dr. Emma. "Are you feeling ill? I can see you right now if you are."

"I feel good," the creature said in a deep growling voice. "It's your doctor's office that's sick. **What makes you think you can run a business?**"

"Who-who are you?" said Dr. Emma, *her voice trembling.*

"Well, all business owners know me. Or they should! I am Grumble. Let me guess. Business isn't going well for you right now. Is it?"

"W-well, no," said Dr. Emma.

Grumble smiled widely and laughed a wicked laugh.

"Tell Grumble all about it."

"I've always wanted to be a doctor. And I've always wanted my own kid business. But now that I have one, I have no patients to treat. I'm here every day, but no one comes in. I don't know what to do."

"I know exactly what you should do," he said with a smirk.
"QUIT! Close your business. Running a business
is too hard for a kid. You'll never succeed.

"Why would you want to be a doctor and spend all day
with sick people, anyway? They're gross.
They cough and sneeze. Just give up now!"

As he spoke, Grumble's words formed ropes that wrapped themselves around Dr. Emma.
The dark clouds above his head grew bigger and darker and made a loud rumble.
Dr. Emma's eyes turned into swirls as if she was being hypnotized.

"Close my business. Close my business," Dr. Emma said again and again. "Yes, I will close my business."

Grumble was turning her into his prisoner.

Just then, a flash of lightning struck the dark clouds above them and snapped the cords into pieces. Dr. Emma shook her head, and her eyes returned to normal.

"Stop right there, Grumble!" shouted Lisa. She ran toward him.

"Oh, no, the Super CEO Girls! Not again!" said Grumble. He formed an even larger dark cloud and hurled it at Lisa, knocking her back.

The Super CEO Girls stormed toward Grumble together this time, hurling their lightning bolts at the dark clouds.

"That's right, Grumble," said Kate. **"You bring the thunder, but we bring the lightning."**

Anna rushed up and grabbed Dr. Emma to get her away from Grumble. Kate shot away the rest of the clouds over Dr. Emma's head. And Lisa formed three huge lightning bolts.

"Courage! Hard work! Creativity!"
she shouted as she shot each lightning bolt at Grumble.

They struck him in the rear. "Yow!!!" shouted Grumble as he ran away.

"Don't worry! You're safe now," Anna said to Dr. Emma as they watched Grumble run into the distance.

"Wow, thank you," said Dr. Emma. "He really made me believe I didn't want to keep my doctor's office. I almost gave up."

Kate tapped her bracelet. A holograph appeared above her arm.

"Wow, what's that?" Dr. Emma asked.

"Oh, that's a Personal Holographic Operational Nano Emitter. But we just call it a P.H.O.N.E. for short," Anna said.

"So, it seems to me that what you have is an advertising problem." Kate checked her calculations. "There are 4.6 million kids in Kidtropolis. They all need checkups, and some of them are even sick and need to see a doctor. **We just need to get the word out.**"

"But how? I don't know what to do. Maybe Grumble was right," Dr. Emma said with a frown.

Anna took Dr. Emma's hand. "Don't worry. We'll help you."

Dr. Emma's eyes lit up. "Will you really help me?"

"Of course, we will!" Lisa said with a grin. **"We're the Super CEO Girls!"**

"When you don't know what to do, ask an expert. Like us. Let's get down to business," said Kate.

Dr. Emma explained all of her problems to the CEOs, and they quickly came up with a solution.

Kate showed Dr. Emma her plan on her P.H.O.N.E.'s hologram screen. "We know just how to fill your piggy bank up and get you lots and lots of patients to see!

"First, you need an ad — which is what I do best," said Kate proudly.

"You mean I need to learn to add? **Like 1 + 1 = 2?**" Dr. Emma asked.

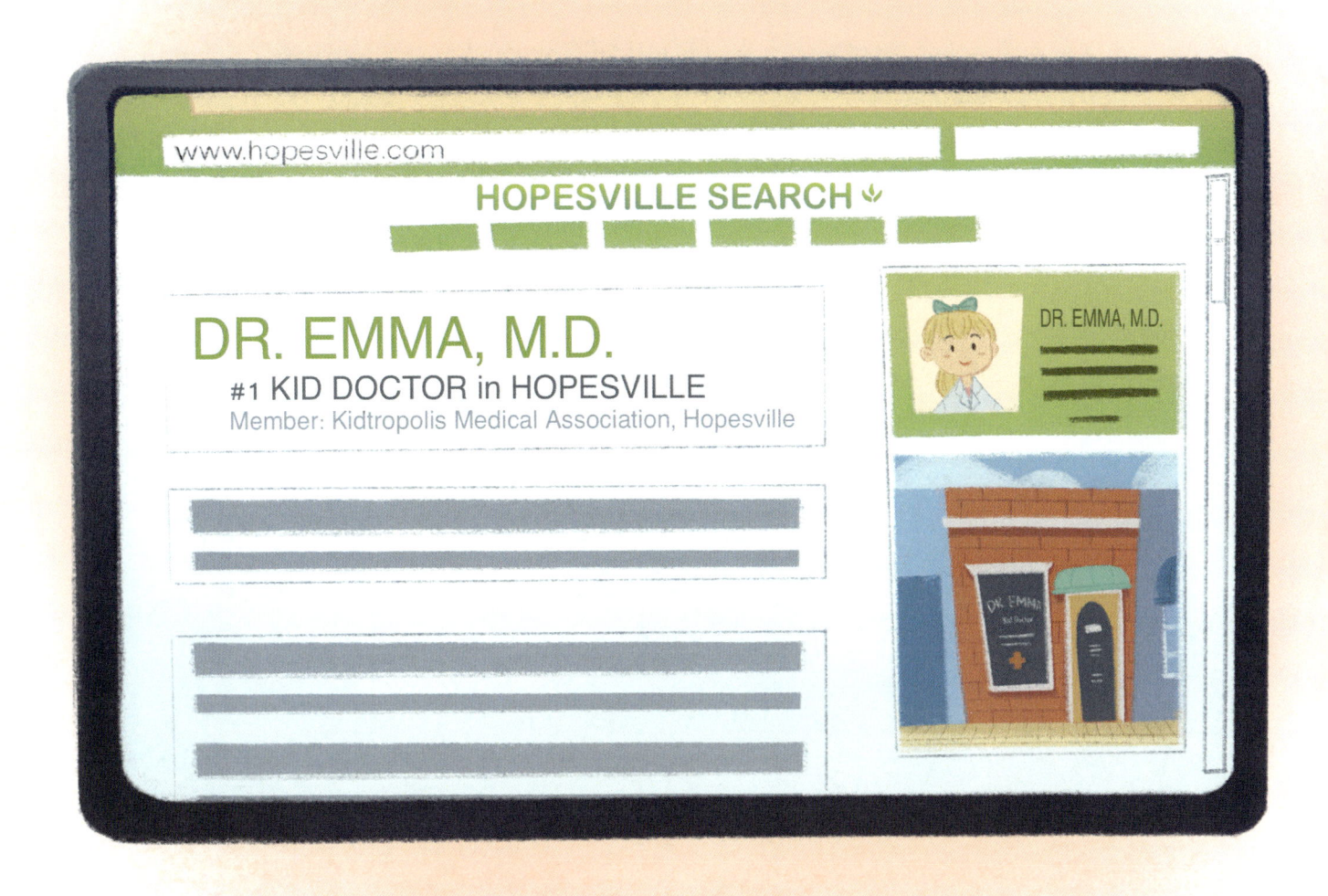

"No. Every day, kids that need a doctor are looking for a 'kid doctor in Hopesville' on the internet. An ad is when you pay money to be at the top of the list."

Kate touched her advertising power bracelet, and a hologram screen instantly showed Dr. Emma's office at the top of a list of doctor's offices in the area.

"Now every kid that needs a doctor will see you first and know you're ready to help them. That's the power of advertising!" Anna clapped with excitement.

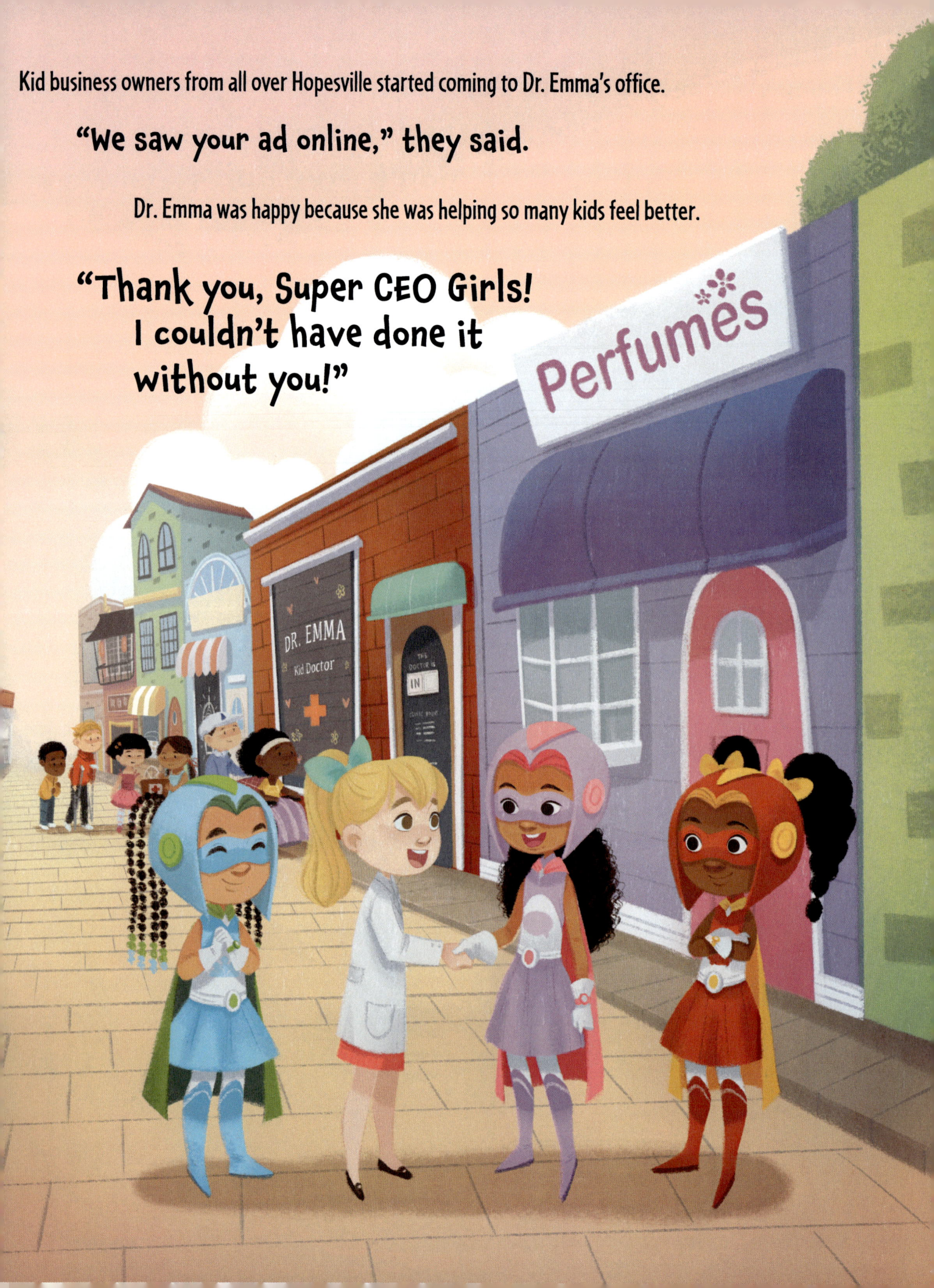

Kid business owners from all over Hopesville started coming to Dr. Emma's office.

"We saw your ad online," they said.

Dr. Emma was happy because she was helping so many kids feel better.

"Thank you, Super CEO Girls! I couldn't have done it without you!"

"If you ever need us again," Kate said,
"just call. And remember . . ." The girls spoke in unison:
"Dream it, do it, don't give up!"

They held hands and shouted:

"Super CEOs.
We're smart, don't you know?
Our bracelets are aglow,
And . . . now . . . it's . . . time . . . to . . . GO!!"

In a burst of lightning, they vanished and made it home just in time for story time with Mom.

Don't Miss the Next Adventure in
The Super CEO Girls™ Series!

Book 2: Treehouse Trouble™

Our heroes are at it again. This time, an industrious builder wants to expand her business. But how can she when she doesn't have the money she needs? And, that dastardly Grumble is at it again, trying to convince kids that they can't do what they've set their minds to! Will Grumble succeed in spreading negative thoughts, or will the Super CEOs defeat his lies and help the business owner figure out how to save her business? The only way to know is to follow our girls on their adventures.

Book 3: Rocky Real Estate™

A young real estate tycoon is having all sorts of problems, and she is just about to give up on her business. To make matters worse, the evil bear, Grumble, is there to convince the young business owner that kids can't succeed in business. Enter our Super CEOs. Kate, Lisa, and Anna fight the mean old bear and try to help our entrepreneur learn how to be successful in business. Will they be able to save another business, or will Grumble's doubts and fears cause the kid to give up? It's another great adventure with Super CEOs!

Book 4: Training Time™

It's time for another great adventure. But our heroes sure do have their hands full, because a kid lawyer is having trouble running her law firm. And sure enough, Grumble is there to spread his special brand of discouragement, ready to stop her from being in business and poised to fight our heroes if they try to help. Will the girls be able to solve this little lawyer's problem? Or will she have to close up shop and give it all up? You simply can't miss this episode of Super CEOs.

Book 5: Money Management Madness!™

It's another great adventure for our Super CEOs. But this time, the kid they want to help doesn't have a business. She has twenty-five businesses! And she is having a hard time figuring out everything she needs to know. Fortunately, the Super CEOs are on the way to save the day. But you know who is on his way too. And he just loves to make kids quit running their businesses. Our girls will have to fight Grumble off and then help our struggling kid entrepreneur get a handle on her business. Can they do it?

Book 6: Risky Business™

Running a business is fun. But what happens when it gets risky? In this thrilling episode, the girls join Mom as she buys a new company. It's a great lesson our heroes learn just in time to help a kid who runs a software engineering firm. Readers will learn about stocks, acquisitions, mergers, and the value of research in terms they can understand with a story they will love.

Book 7: Piggy Bank Problems™

Our superheroes are exploring the world of charity. They are learning about the ways in which communities come together to help those in need. But, even while doing charity, they can find time to help a kid entrepreneur in need. They find a kid who is running a charity to help the less fortunate. But even a business that is concerned solely with helping others sometimes needs help itself. And the Super CEO Girls™ are there to save the day. Topics such as foundations, charities, and nonprofits are on the menu for this heaping serving of Super CEOs.

Book 8: The Cure for Doubt™

We get a rare look into the home of our dastardly devil, Grumble, in this edition of the Super CEO Girls™. And he has something especially sinister on his mind. In the meantime, our girls are celebrating Mom's business success at the top of a high-rise office building when they get a call to help a kid in need. When they arrive in Kidtropolis, what they find is something they have never dealt with before. But, as usual, the Super CEOs are always ready with the help kids need to succeed. And, as usual, Grumble is there to spread lies, fear, and doubt. Just wait until you learn how the Super CEOs handle this challenge.

Book 9: Start-Up Slip Up™

Our Super CEO Girls™ are learning more and more about business as they watch their parents make a big deal. In this edition, our girls are visiting the New York Stock Exchange for the first time and learning about the process of turning a start-up business into a success. But even a great event like this won't stop them from helping kids who need them. And the kid who needs them has the oldest problem in the book: she has run out of money. Can our Super CEOs figure out how to help the kid entrepreneur get the money she needs to keep her new business running and help it to grow? Stay tuned to every exciting page and see how Grumble gets a taste of his own medicine.

Book 10: The Case of the Bashful Boss™

It's a special day in the Kingston home as a presidential candidate and a few dozen other people stop by for dinner. Our girls trade their superhero suits for fancy dresses. But they would never trade the important work of saving businesses from mean old Grumble's lies. They meet a lot of kids who need a lot of help. And, of course, who is there to stop them all? Grumble. Will the Super CEOs be able to help so many kids at once? And whatever will they do with that bear who has a few new tricks up his sleeve? You don't want to miss this edition of the Super CEO Girls™.

For more information, please visit:
www.superceogirls.com